Originally published as *Jij bent bijzonder* in Belgium and the Netherlands by Clavis Uitgeverij, 2019
English translation from the Dutch by Clavis Publishing Inc., New York

Visit us on the Web at www.clavis-publishing.com.

You Are Special written and illustrated by Sam Loman

ISBN 978-1-60537-532-8

This book was printed in January 2020 at Nikara, M. R. Štefánika 858/25, 963 01 Krupina, Slovakia.

First Edition
10 9 8 7 6 5 4 3 2 1

YOU ARE SPECIAL

Clavis

NEW YORK

by Sam Loman

Kiki looks in the mirror.

She examines herself from all angles.

"My fur is so boring," she sighs.

"I wish I had *beautiful* colors, just like my friends.

Then I would be very special."

Then Kiki has an idea.
She takes a big red pencil
and uses it to draw RED squares on her ears.

"Hello, Ladybug," Kiki says.
"How do you like my ears?"
"They're okay," says Ladybug.
And then she flies away.

Maybe I need more colors, Kiki thinks.

She draws ORANGE circles on her legs.

"Hello, Butterfly," she says.
"How do you like my orange legs?"
But before she even gets an answer,
Butterfly has flown off.

"Maybe some yellow?"
Kiki puts her paw
in some YELLOW paint.

"Hello, Giraffe. How do I look?" Kiki asks.

"Pretty," Giraffe mumbles.

"But you're not even looking!" Kiki says, disappointed.

So Kiki dips her tail in the GREEN paint.

"Tell me, Frog," she says.

"What do you think?"

"About what?" Frog asks, and hops away.

"Oh, never mind," Kiki sighs.

Kiki draws some big **BLUE** circles on her face.

"Aren't I pretty?" she asks Peacock.
"Well, you aren't as pretty as I am,"
says Peacock as he spreads his feathers.

Kiki decides to draw PINK stripes on her belly.

"Very nice," Piglet calls from the swing.
"Nice?" Kiki gulps. Nice isn't good enough!
She wants to be special.

Kiki walks away in a huff
and doesn't notice the paint cans . . .
Smack! Splatter! Splosh!
Kiki looks at her fur.
Oh, dear—she is completely
covered in PURPLE paint!

"Wow, you're purple!" someone says.
Kiki notices another purple cat.
It's her brother, Goof.

Kiki smiles. "Look, we are both purple now.
But don't you think we will be more
special if we had lots of colors?"
"Let's do it!" says Goof.

Goof picks  GREEN, YELLOW, RED, and BLUE.

Kiki adds some pink and orange stripes to her tail.

"We are the prettiest animals in the world," they agree. But it's time to go home.

"Mommy!" Goof calls.

"Don't we look special?"

"You look like two rainbows," Mommy says with a smile.

"Not special?" Kiki asks.

"Very special," Mommy says.

"But you are special just the way you are.
Now into the bath, you two!" says Mommy.

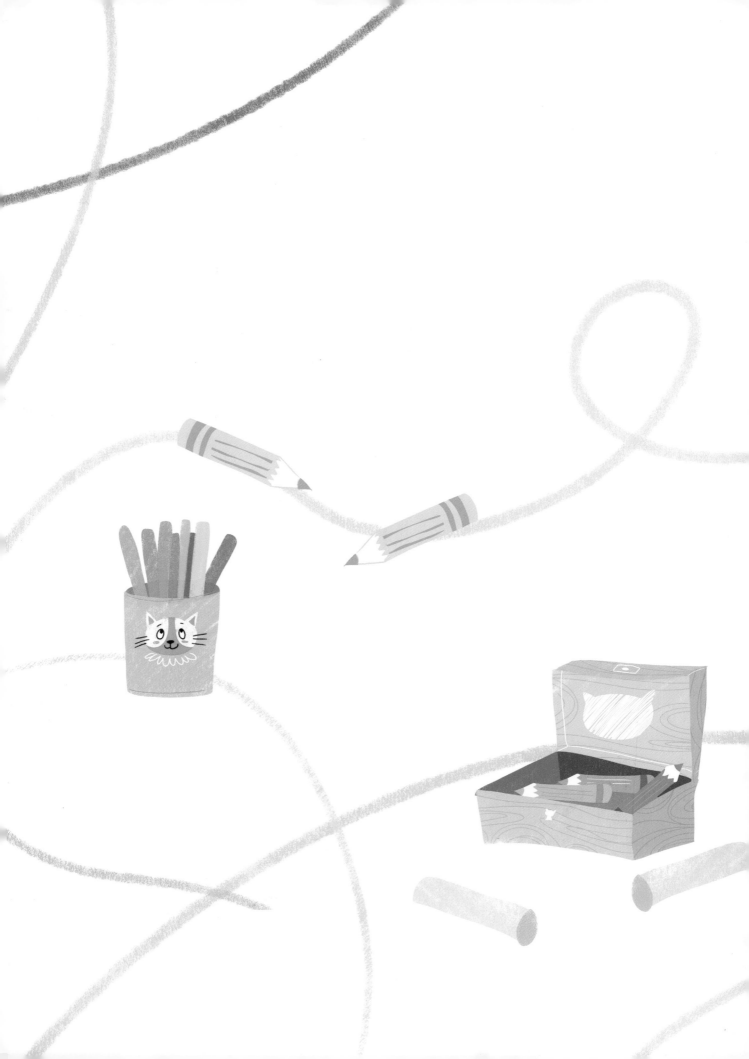